The Spiky Ste

Adapted by Andrea Posner-Sanchez
from the episode "A Spiky Tail Tale"

Based on the television series created by Craig Bartlett

Illustrated by Dave Aikins

A GOLDEN BOOK • NEW YORK

randomhouse.com/kids

pbskids.org/dinosaurtrain

ISBN: 978-0-307-93022-4

Printed in the United States of America

10 9 8 7 6 5 4 3 2 1

THE JIM HENSON COMPANY

www.henson.com

One sunny morning, Tiny and Buddy were taking turns imitating different kinds of dinosaurs. Tiny was pretending to be a Stegosaurus.

"I walk on four legs. I have plates on my back and spikes on my tail," she said. "I use my tail spikes to . . . um . . . carry food around, or . . . um . . . to cool off my body."

Buddy didn't think that sounded right.

Buddy thought of their friend Morris the Stegosaurus. "Morris's spikes go off to the side, not up and down like the plates on his back," he told his sister. "They probably don't cool him."

"They could still catch a breeze!" argued Tiny.

"I don't think they do!" Buddy argued back.

Buddy and Tiny's mom heard the arguing and came right over. She didn't know what Morris Stegosaurus used his spikes for, either.

"Let's visit Morris and ask him," Mrs. Pteranodon suggested.

"Hooray!" shouted Buddy and Tiny.

Mr. Conductor greeted
the Pteranodon family at the
train station. "All aboard the
Dinosaur Train!" he said.

On the train, Mr. Conductor showed Buddy and Tiny a picture of a Stegosaurus.

"See, the spikes stick out to the side," Buddy pointed out.

"But they don't go straight out," insisted Tiny.

Mr. Conductor told them that going to visit Morris was a very smart thing to do. "Asking questions is a great way to find answers."

Soon the train arrived at Stegosaurus Forest.
As Buddy, Tiny, and Mrs. Pteranodon walked
around looking for their friend, they heard voices.
Morris and another dinosaur were arguing. The
Pteranodons rushed toward the sounds.

Morris Stegosaurus and Alvin Allosaurus were standing on opposite sides of a gully. They did not look happy.

"This is my gully, man," said Morris. "And I want to go to that side for the tasty plants."

"Ha! This is my gully," Alvin said. "You better stay away from me, and let me go to that side to find some good meat to eat."

The two dinosaurs didn't seem to like each other at all.

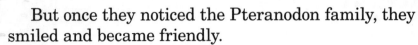

But once they noticed the Pteranodon family, they smiled and became friendly.

"Awesome to see you guys!" Morris said.

"What are you two arguing about?" asked Buddy.

Morris and Alvin explained that they had never been friends. After all, Allosaurus were predators. They were always trying to catch Stegosaurus.

"But maybe you two could *become* friends,"
Tiny suggested.
"Nah!" they said, shaking their heads.

Buddy thought for a second. "Well, we can at least figure out how each of you can get to the other side of the gully without fighting," he said.

"Great idea!" said Mrs. Pteranodon.

Suddenly, Alvin took a step toward the center of the gully.

"Whoa! Stay on your side," Morris yelled as he whipped his tail around.

Alvin jumped away. "Man, that is one dangerous tail!" he said.

Then Buddy and Tiny remembered the reason for their visit.

"Morris, Tiny and I were arguing about what you use your spiky tail for," said Buddy.

"Does your spiky tail help you cool down at all?" asked Tiny.

"Naw, the plates on my back do that," Morris answered.

Tiny had another question. "Do you ever carry food on your spikes?"

"I've never carried anything on my spikes. Awesome idea, though," said Morris.

Buddy and Tiny lightly touched Morris's spikes.

"Very spiky!" they agreed.

"My tail helps me protect myself," explained Morris. "I'd never hurt you kids with my spiky tail. But it does keep predators away, if you know what I mean."

Just then, Morris noticed that Alvin was standing a little too close for comfort. Morris whipped his spiky tail around.

"Hey! I was just looking," said Alvin, jumping back. "I've always been afraid of Morris's spikes, so I avoid them by moving really fast," he explained to Buddy and Tiny.

The Pteranodons stepped away for a quick family meeting. "Alvin and Morris are natural enemies. They'll never be best friends," Mrs. Pteranodon told Buddy and Tiny.

"But maybe we can convince them to try to get along," Tiny suggested.

Tiny and Buddy approached the big dinosaurs.

"If you switch sides of the gully, Morris gets his tasty ferns," Tiny said.

"And Alvin gets his meat," continued Buddy. "So do you want to work together and switch?"

Alvin and Morris agreed to give it a try.

Tiny told Alvin and Morris to each take a big step to their right. "Now walk forward."

Buddy reminded both dinosaurs not to swing their tails too much.

"You did it!" shouted Tiny.

"And no one got spiked!" added Buddy.

Alvin and Morris were happy. They even agreed to stop fighting and start being friendly to each other.

Buddy and Tiny realized that they had been fighting, too.

"I'm sorry I argued with you about what Morris's tail spikes were for," Buddy told his sister.

"I'm sorry, too," said Tiny. "I sure know one thing—you're my best friend, Buddy!"